Holiday Stew

by

Jenny Whitehead

Henry Holt and Company
New York

Though every year was different,
Our holidays still came
traditionally,
unconditionally,
delightfully the same.
Through many changing seasons
I think of all we had,
And lovingly,
contentedly,
I thank my Mom and Dad.

Henry Holt and Company, LLC
Publishers since 1866
175 Fifth Avenue, New York, New York 10010
www.henryholtchildrensbooks.com

Henry Holt® is a registered trademark of
Henry Holt and Company, LLC.
Copyright © 2007 by Jenny Whitehead
All rights reserved.
Distributed in Canada by H. B. Fenn and Company Ltd.

Library of Congress Cataloging-in-Publication Data
Whitehead, Jenny.
Holiday stew: a kid's portion of holiday
and seasonal poems / Jenny Whitehead.—1st ed.
p.   cm.
ISBN-13: 978-0-8050-7715-5 / ISBN-10: 0-8050-7715-4
1. Holidays—Juvenile poetry. 2. Children's poetry. I. Title.
PS3573.H4815H65 2007 811'.6—dc22 2006011144

The artist used gouache and black pen line on Arches 90-lb.
hot-press paper to create the illustrations for this book.

First Edition—2007
Printed in China on acid-free paper. ∞

1 3 5 7 9 10 8 6 4 2

thanks, Christy!

Contents

Spring (Begins March 20 or 21)

Summer (Begins June 20 or 21)

July

August

September

School

October

November

December

Contents Cont.

Fall (Begins September 22 or 23)

Winter (Begins December 21 or 22)

The Wind invited Kite and Flag to play. "I'm it!" Wind said and chased them both all day.

Spring Fever!

Here I go again—
ACHOO!
What do I have?
Spring fever?
Flu?
It's in the air.
It's up my—
SNEEZE!
I remember—
allergies!

ACHOoooo

Worm Talk

You may *think*
that worms
like puddles
since we come out
when it rains.
But my home
is underground
so I'm just waiting
till it drains.

Yellow slicker, tell me why, you still look wet when you are dry?

6

If I Could Paint a Springtime Day

If I could paint a springtime day,
I'd dip my brush in rain,
And splatter pink the popcorn trees
That bloom along the lane.

I'd mix a shade of purple
Chilled from one last winter snow,
To decorate the crocuses;
Brave soldiers in a row.

And when the sun peeks out,
I'd catch some yellow in my hand,
And finger-paint forsythia
To wake the dreary land.

And then I'd borrow emerald green
From seedlings breaking through,
And paint a thousand blades of grass
To hold the summer's dew.

Last, I'd tint the tulips
Gently waking in their bed,
And welcome home the robin—
Painted breast, a splendid red.

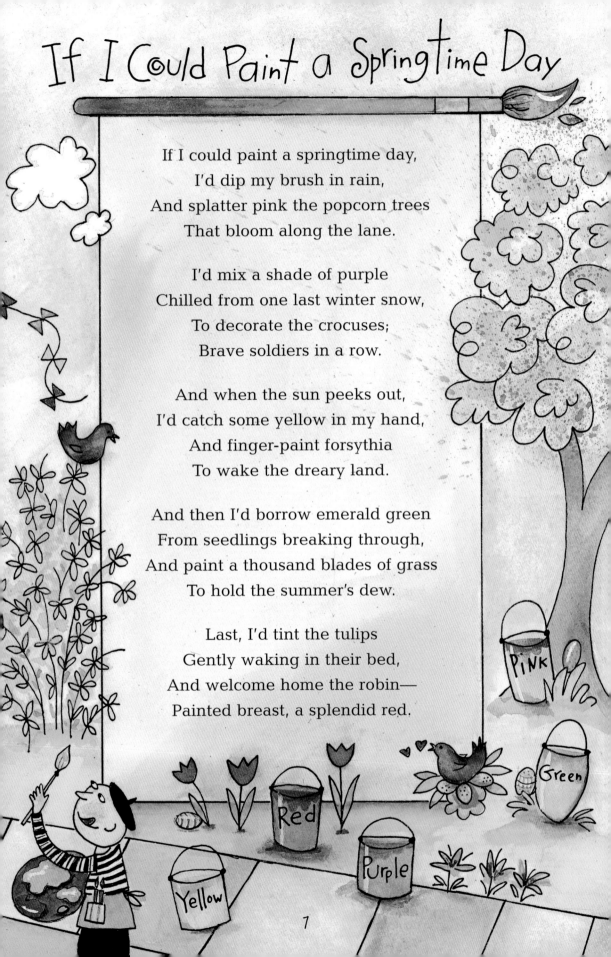

Pink

Green

Red

Purple

Yellow

Spring-Cleaning the City!

Patching up the potholes,
  Scrubbing statues white,
Sweeping up the brown leaves,
  Buffing buildings bright,
Turning on the fountains,
  Washing down the street,
Spring-cleaning the city
  Is finally complete!

8

On St. Patrick's Day

March 17

Read with an Irish brogue!

A "Top of the Morning!"
Child, where is your green?
From my head to my feet,
I am green in between!
Got my leprechaun hat
And my shamrock balloon,
'Tis an Irish parade
Passing by here at noon.
Aye, soda bread's baking,
Corned beef's in the pot,
I'm dancing a jig—
My feet, they won't stop!
A toast to good health—
Lift your green milk—*SLAINTE!*
Not Irish? No matter . . .
Ye're Irish today!

Soda Bread

Corned beef and cabbage

Top of the Mornin' to you!

* Slainte sounds like 'Slawn-chā' and means "To Your Health!"

9

Questions Are Welcome

(A Passover Poem)

"Why is this night not like other nights?"
"Why do we eat bread that's so flat?"
"Why do we dip greens in a salt-water cup?"
"There's a bone and an egg. Why is that?"

My questions are welcomed at our Seder meal
Where the Passover story is told.
Our Jewish traditions are still new to me,
But the answers—three thousand years old.

Happy Easter Mornin'

A Sunday in March or April

Our basket's over-flowin'!
White shiny shoes are glowin'!
A feast is in the making!
God's Son is re-awaking!
Church bells are a-ringing!
There's Alleluia-singing!
The Easter lily's swaying!
All Christians are a-praying!
There's no more Lent-forlornin'!
It's "Happy Easter Mornin'"!

An Easter Egg

Bright

GOT IT!   white
hide   boiled
shell   blotted
swell   dipped
spotted   dripped
        tinted

APRIL FOOLS' DAY!

A trick by a friend,
a prank by a brother
pales dearly compared
to one planned by your mother.

She's plotted all year
while she scraped, scoured, and scrubbed
your grass stains, your grease stains,
your grimy-ringed tub.

She may try to set
your alarm clock ahead,
so you're washed and dressed
while the world's still in bed.

Or lovingly make
your ham sandwich for school
with paper, not cheese,
that reads "April Fools!"

But lucky for us
on this one single day,
a trick on your mother
is also okay.

So, no one will blame you—
it won't be your fault.
The sugar-bowl sugar's not sugar—
it's SALT!

The Clock's Gone Cuckoo!
(A Daylight Savings Poem)

gain an hour? **13**

~~12~~

lose an hour?

11

I'm confused!

10

9

They say we lost an hour.
I'm not sure where it went.
Our clocks are all mixed up—
My head feels like cement.

Down the stairs I stumble—
Hey, who turned on the sun?
Dad's newspaper is sideways,
His shave is halfway done.

Look! Mom's pouring cat food
In all our breakfast bowls.
My sister's twisted sweater
Has mismatched buttonholes!

Luckily, this strange time change
Starts quietly on Sunday.
Imagine what could happen
If it started on a Monday!

News

1st Sunday in APRIL

Spring → Forward

Cat Food

Mother Earth

Mother Earth has brown skin—
With hair of swaying wheat,
Her snow-white teeth are mountain caps,
Her heart, the lava heat.
She sewed her dress from farmers' fields,
She topped her hat with gourds.
Her tummy rumbles quietly,
She shifts when she is bored.
She blushes when the sun rises
And hides during an eclipse.
The wind is but a sigh from her,
The rivers are her lips.
She's older than the oldest tree
And softer than the sand,
She'll be here for us always,
If we gently hold her hand.

A Little Litter Poem

I play a little litter game
and pick up trash I find.
I like to turn around and see
the clean I've left behind.

Thanks, Mister Kid!

TRASH

14

Plant Some Trees on ARBOR DAY

Last week in April

start here

The trees I draw
are lollipops.
I'll plant some sticks
and grow the tops.

then zig-zag!

I'll put a seed
under the shed.
A tree-house tree
may grow instead.

I'll dig up holes
for dogwood trees
and grow some puppies
without fleas.

Home sweet Home

A No-Flea Tree

hi

My family tree
I'll water well—
another cousin
would be swell.

I won't forget
maples and oaks.
I'll grow fresh air
for other folks.

Tree Seeds

Our Earth needs trees
of every kind—
what kind of tree
will you leave behind?

15

Did You Bring Spring?
(A May Day Poem)

I hear a knock!
Who can it be?

(We flee!)

Gee!

Little
flowers,
Paper bee!
For me?

Oh, glee!

How
I wish
that you could see
how
happy,
HAPPY
you've made me!

(We see!)

16

It's Cinco de Mayo!
(in a Mexican Hat Dance Style)

¡Cantar! (Sing poem)

A long, long time ago (CLAP! CLAP!)
A town in Mexico (CLAP! CLAP!)
Fought hard for liberty (CLAP! CLAP!)
Then Mexico was free! (CLAP! CLAP!)

Sooo, girls, put on dresses with ruffles on ruffles,
And, boys, show your Mexican roots with your boots,
Throw down your sombreros, and pound with your feet
To the fast mariachi band beat.

Castillos light the night (CLAP! CLAP!)
Tortillas taste just right (CLAP! CLAP!)
Hooray for Fifth of May (CLAP! CLAP!)
Fiesta fun all day!

OLÉ!

Breakfast in Bed
For Mother's Day!

We cooked Mom scrambled eggs
(and dropped some on the floor).

We made her buttered toast
(and smeared the kitchen door).

We flipped a dozen pancakes
(now two are on the ceiling).

We sliced up a banana
(I think we lost the peeling).

We poured the maple syrup
(it's dripping down the chairs).

Happy Mother's Day, Mom.
(Well, *if* you stay upstairs!)

Remembering on Memorial Day

I remembered that school was closed for the day.
I remembered the fairgrounds and fire-truck spray.
I remembered the picnic and horseshoes we tossed.
Then I remembered to remember the heroes we've lost.

Air Force — Navy — Coast Guard — National Guard — Marines — Army

The Sprinkler (some COOL before the POOL... ...opens!)

I crank up the faucet
As high as it goes.
PSSFT! Water sputters
Its way through the hose.
The warm trickle's fickle;
The cold must push through—
I'm waiting...I'm waiting...
Then *ch-ch-ch-shoo!*

The sprinkler's alive!
It dances! It jumps!
It chases us with
Every gallon it pumps.
We race back and forth,
Ahead of it, then
We turn and run through it
Again and again.

In the Heat of the Game

I can eat a HOT hot dog,
sweat the stadium heat.
I can peel my thighs off
this—OUCH!—bleacher seat.

Yes, only ONE thing
at a game makes me blister.
It's the foul ball that's caught
not by me, but my sister!
UGH!

The Gnat

I swing I swing I swing the bat.
I miss the ball and hit a gnat.
The ball, it lands right on my toe.
The gnat lands on first base—Gnat, GO!
It flies from second to third base,
Then rounds it home—we won! First place!
But gnats are way too small to see
So no one knows we won but me.

Summer Groove

Do the hop-hopscotch,
Move those hula-hula hips,
Pump the swing-swing swoop,
Bounce your boing-boing flips,
Splish your splash in the pool,
Twirl-y whirl till you tip,
Jump-a jump-a jump a rope,
Breathe a breath—
Slurp a sip!

Sleepover Fun

It's just about midnight.
Let's stay up till two.
We're all wide awake
And there's still more to do.

Pass the pillow, the polish,
And cheese popcorn, please.
We'll watch one more movie,
Tell secrets and . . . zzzzzzzzs.

23

Lightning bugs tease us for fun—
They make us run - stop - run - stop - run!

Camping

In the middle of the night
In a campground, wide awake,
Watch the dipper spilling stars,
Hear the water-lapping lake,
Smell the ember rubble cooling,
Taste the s'more still in your teeth,
Feel the warmth of flannel blankets
As you burrow underneath.

Going Fishing

You bring the pole,
I'll find the bait.
You rent the boat,
I'll get the plate.
You hook the worm,
I'll catch the fish.
You start the fire,
I'll clean the dish.

For Father's Day

3rd Sunday in June

#1 Coupon for Dad------
I could straighten your toolbox,
Wax your new car,
And dust every CD you own.
OR turn in this coupon
For your guarantee—
I'll leave all your good stuff alone!

#2 Coupon for DAD----
A Father's Day sandwich I'll make by myself
With food I can reach from the fridge bottom shelf.

#3 Coupon for DAD--------
Good for one "Daddy Day" makeover splurge
Here, at the Bathroom Salon.
We'll poof, pluck, and puff,
Trim, shampoo, and buff,
And paint your nails Bright-Pink Chiffon.

Bathroom SALON

#4 Coupon for DAD---
This coupon's a ticket to My Dad,
A musical tribute for you.
I'll blow my trumpet and tap dance,
Burp songs and play the kazoo.

#5 Coupon for DAD
Coffee,
Paper,
Favorite chair,
TV sports,
And nap . . .
Peace and quiet,
Reading books,
And me
In your lap.

I ♥ DAD

The Flower Party

(Find 18 flowers in the poem.)
Answers- next page!

Swish swish fiddle dee bop—
What could be that sound?
I think I see a flower party
Down there on the ground!
Watch those lolli-poppies cha-cha,
Teasing all the bees,
And silly dilly daffy-dillies
Giggle in the breeze.
Now dandy-lion puff buffs up
His merry gold-tipped shoes,
While jazzmen use two lips to blow
Some thistle whistle blues.

hee
hee

WOW!

It's four o'clock—*ding, ding, ding, ding.*
Hear all the blue bells ring?
Time for tea in buttered cups
While Lily Valley sings!
Look! A dressed-up-snappy dragon
In bright lilac pants
Asking blushing Rose
To do a 1-2-3 swing dance.
They stop to catch their baby's breath—
Can can they dance again?
Oh, yes! All day see wild flowers
Bob like chicks and hens.

Hello. I'm Mary Gold!

Answers

hen and chicks
wildflowers
daisies
baby's breath
roses
lilacs
snapdragons
lily-of-the-valleys
buttercups
bluebells
four-o'clocks
thistles
tulips
jasmines
marigolds
dandelions
daffodils
poppies

CAMP-A-LOT

Dear Mom and Dad,

I'm having fun at summer camp.
Besides the bites and swimmer's cramp,
I carved a fine potato stamp.

We've hiked and knotted macramé.
I painted pots and threw some clay.
(Don't worry, they said that's okay!)

I'm eating almost every dish,
But not meatballs—they taste like fish,
And not the fish—it's rubber-ish.

I'm making friends and sleeping well,
The ghost stories they tell are swell,
And no one minds we kind of smell.

I better go! It's almost three
And time for our camp jamboree.
I miss you like I miss TV (and that's a lot!).

Love, SAM

whooo wants a care package?

We do!

Send nuts (and gum for the Kid).

Beach Souvenirs

I brought home some taffy and tropical fruit,
some freckles, a sunburn, and sand in my suit.
I wanted to bring home the ocean as well,
so, Dad, let me take the waves back in this shell.

For Flag Day

June 14th

A flip-flapping flag
is telling its story
Of freedom and fighting
and honor and glory.
The stars and the stripes
have so much to say,
So let them keep talking
through Veterans Day!

Who Invited Insects to Our Picnic?

Who invited insects to our picnic?
Bugs are now arriving rather quick quick.
They are hungry, they are rude.
They are stealing all our food.
I say, who invited insects to our picnic?

Who Invited People to Our Picnic?

Who invited people to our picnic?
Won't they ever leave so we can pick pick?
They are noisy, they are tall.
They brush crumbs down on us all.
Why thanks, people, for coming to our picnic!

At the End of the Day...
(A Fourth of July poem)

At the end of the day
When you've seen the parade
And eaten your last piece of pie,
Remember the fun's just begun
If the end of the day's
On the Fourth of July!
Sooo . . .

. . . Grab your blankets!
Lift your chins!
It's getting dark—
The show begins!

Climbing color . . .
Waiting . . . *BURST!*
A brilliant bowl
Of yellow first.

Splendid poofs
Of glitter gold,
Bring oohs and ahhs
From young and old.

Silver sizzles,
Rockets soar.
Crowds are cheering,
Trumpets roar.

Night bright
Like a chandelier—
POOF!—shut off
Until next year.

AUGUST 3

For Friendship Day

A good friend . . .

. . . helps you poke things with a stick,

. . . brings home homework when you're sick,

. . . calls you first on snow-day days,

. . . knows you don't like "mayo-naise,"

. . . stops your skateboard when you fall,

. . . forgets you didn't catch the ball,

. . . sends you postcards on a trip,

. . . whispers "*psst*—milk on your lip,"

. . . makes you laugh when you should not
(even though you might get caught!).

A *best* friend . . .

. . . knows your shrug, your snort, your pout,
and still likes you inside out.

Hi! It's me.. ho WAY!

Cookie dough!

How annoying!

Wow!

O.K.

Bye!

Friends 4 eVer

The Last Leaf

Hooray! At last, it's my turn!
I let go of the tree.
I dive, I flip, I double twist,
In case you're watching me.

I back float on the wind awhile,
Then do the swimmer's crawl.
How kind of you to rake a pile
Of leaves to break my fall.

I wish I never had to land
But I will be there soon.
Then you and I and our leaf friends
Can play all afternoon.

A Recipe for Fall Pie

Press cicada wings in pie pan,
Fill with pumpkin guts galore.
Squish squash, peas, turnips, and cabbage,
Mix with milkweed pods, and pour.
Sprinkle crinkled leaves and cover,
Cook an hour in low sun.
Offer piece to little brother.
    (When he tastes it, better run!)

Old Cicada Wings

Fresh-from-the-Ground Squash and Cabbage

Milk-weed pods

Jumbo Pack O' Turnips

~ Hello, Scarecrow, full of thatch,
If I were you, I'd have to scratch!

Bear Crossing

Just like a bear
I ate and ate,
then went to bed
to hibernate.
If you start to
wake me—wait!
I growl if I can't
sleep in late!

Let's Go On a Hayride

The harvest moon's rising,
So climb aboard, friends—
Our hayride's about to begin.
After you've covered your toes with the straw,
Pull the blankets up under your chin.

Aye, giddyup, Tumbleweed!
Giddyup, Skip!
Lead our wagon up over the hill.
Now, look to your left, there's a deer in the wood,
And above you, a brown whippoorwill . . .

Trot! Trot! Hold on tight
As we ride down the trail.
Hear the crackle of leaves on the ground?
And, listen, the cackle of geese heading south
Is, to me, the most wonderful sound.

We'll head by the pond
And then back to the barn.
It feels like it's ready to snow.
Do you smell the bonfire waiting for us?
Here we are! Slow down, horses.
Whoa! Whoa!

Farmer Firefighter Accountant Doctor Builder

1st Monday in September

It's Labor Day

A holiday for hard work?
Yes, grown-ups, you deserve it!
But thank you very kindly
For letting kids observe it.

Our school year's just beginning,
All summer we've slept late.
The only job we worked at
Was playing three months straight!

So, to make it fair for you,
We'll work on Labor Day.
Our job? To let you sleep in,
And then make sure you play!

shh

Postal Worker Banker Dog Groomer Baker Plumber

It's Grandma-Grandpa-Nana-Pop-Pop-Granddad Day!

Hi, Grandma, come play!
It's Grandparents' Day!
I've planned some fun things to do—
   We'll dress up like spies,
      Make chocolate mud pies,
         And give my dog a shampoo.
We'll papier-mâché,
      . . . *Baking cookies*, you say?
OR I can come visit you!

1st Sunday after Labor Day

I like spaghetti. Do you?

No, I like toast.

Goofy Grandpa!

Can a puppy-puppet talk?
Can a coin come out my ear?
Can a horse trot through the house?
Can a real genie appear?
Can a big kid learn to polka?
Can a small kid fly a broom?
Don't be silly, yes, of course—
If my grandpa's in the room!

A Long-Distance Connection

Phone call hugs,
Fridge photo smiles,
Traveling for miles and miles;
In a car, letter, or thought—
Nana visits me a lot!

Dear . . .

Miss You! Love, Nana

To:
1 Great
KID
USA

I love you
xo xo

October 12

W

Niña

Pinta

Santa Maria

Scenic route to China

Next rest stop 4000 miles

For Columbus Day

"I'll find the East by sailing west,"
Columbus told the queen.
Three ships followed the setting sun—
A path of tangerine.
Before they reached the edge of earth,
The ocean turned to green.
They found a land, not East or West,
But right here, in between.

It's Rosh Hashanah!

1st and 2nd Days of the Hebrew month of Tishri

Prayer Book

Risen with raisins,
Braided, then baked,
The challah bread's ready to eat.

Dip it in honey,
Wish *Shanah Tova*,
And your New Year will be as sweet!

Let's Blow the Shofar

Halloween Leftovers

You've sifted and sorted,
You've gobbled and hoarded,
The best of your Halloween treats.
What's left, I'm afraid,
You can't even trade
With your sister who likes to eat beets.
But throw it away?
It's still candy—no way!
So what do you do with the stash?
Toss it in a pan,
With corn from a can,
And make leftover Halloween Hash!
Or use candy-corn mix,
And make pot pie for six
In a crust of old 3 Musketeers.
No need to explain,
Your mom can't complain—
She does it with turkey each year!

41

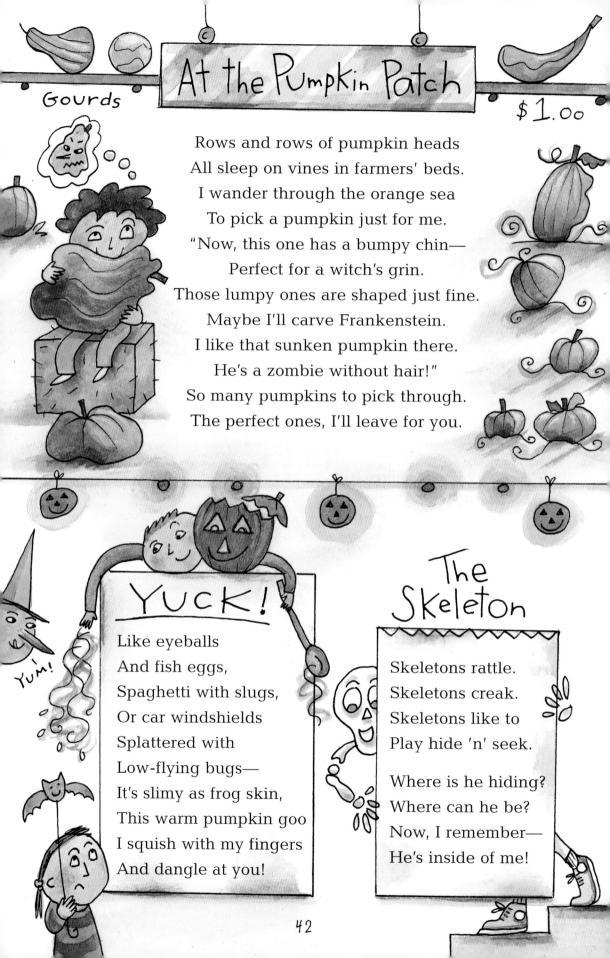

At the Pumpkin Patch

Gourds

$1.00

Rows and rows of pumpkin heads
All sleep on vines in farmers' beds.
I wander through the orange sea
To pick a pumpkin just for me.
"Now, this one has a bumpy chin—
Perfect for a witch's grin.
Those lumpy ones are shaped just fine.
Maybe I'll carve Frankenstein.
I like that sunken pumpkin there.
He's a zombie without hair!"
So many pumpkins to pick through.
The perfect ones, I'll leave for you.

Yum!

YUCK!

Like eyeballs
And fish eggs,
Spaghetti with slugs,
Or car windshields
Splattered with
Low-flying bugs—
It's slimy as frog skin,
This warm pumpkin goo
I squish with my fingers
And dangle at you!

The Skeleton

Skeletons rattle.
Skeletons creak.
Skeletons like to
Play hide 'n' seek.

Where is he hiding?
Where can he be?
Now, I remember—
He's inside of me!

Make Your Costume!

A costume you make
Is one custom-designed,
No store sells the kind
You can find in your mind.

A big-headed monster?
Mix paper and glue,
Then papier-mâché
Not one head, but two!

A blinking-box robot?
A stringy-haired witch?
Just hunt, find, and borrow,
Then glue, paint, or stitch!

A Veterans Day March

Sing it, soldiers— rat-tat-tat, sing it, soldiers— just like that!

Hut–two–three–four.

Army, Air Force, Marine Corps,
Coast Guard, Navy, shore to shore.

Left–right–left–right.

You kept nations safe and free,
bravely fighting tyranny.

Forward march!

Loyal, dedicated, strong!
Home, at last, where you belong.

Attention! Company, halt!

We salute you on this day
with each flag that we display.

At ease.

Army   Air Force   Marines   Coast Guard   Navy

A Thanksgiving Day Quiz

PLEASE ANSWER TRUE OR FALSE:

1. Long ago, way back in May,
    a flowered ship arrived one day.
    T or F

2. The Pilgrims landed by a dock,
    then drove their Plymouth to a rock.
    T or F

3. Pilgrim kids, like us, agree,
    "No giblets in ye recipe!"
    T or F

Ick!

blech!

4. Plant a kernel of corn and a fish in a hole,
    and the corn-covered stalk will grow tall as a pole.
    T or F

5. Native dads taught Pilgrim pops
    to pop popcorn with corncob crops.
    T or F

6. Thanksgiving is the holiday
    when Americans remember
    to thank God for their blessings
    on a Monday in September.
    T or F

Fourth Thursday in November, Silly!

(Answers: 1. F, 2. F, 3. T, 4. T, 5. T, 6. F.)

Stuffed from Head to Toe

Did you gobble gobble turkey?
Did you nibble yibble yams?
Is your tummy feeling crummy
From too many rolls with jam?
Well, wave away the gravy.
Pass politely on the peas.
Then you can save a space for pie
Between your toes and knees.

45

Send Up Some Gratitude

In a time when we all want
a little more–more–more,
stop and think–think–think
of all you're thankful for.
Your mom, your dad—
can you think of any others?
It's okay if you say
your sisters or your brothers.

Good friends, good health,
good luck, good food—
for the good in your life,
send up some gratitude.
For a roof where you live,
for your dog, fish, or bird,
make your thank–thank–thank–you
on Thanksgiving Day be heard!

Wishbone Poem

Pinkies poised up in the air.
We're ready! We're ready!
Make a wish no one can hear.
Be steady! Be steady!
Bend the turkey souvenir.
It's snapping! It's snapping!
Crack! I have the bigger half.
I'm clapping! I'm *clapping*!

Winter

I have but one wish—that you'll join me for fish.

December
January
February

A taste of snowflake on your tongue means wintertime has just begun.

Upside-Down Thinking

I think it's kind of funny
when my nose is cold and runny,
in Australia it is sunny,
warm, and dry.
But while I swim in the pool,
in Australia it is cool.
There, it's winter in the middle
of July!

Winter in the South
(by a kid from the North)

How do you make a snowman
when there isn't any snow?
How do you have a snowball fight
when it melts before you throw?
How do you make snow angels
with green grass on the ground?
You can't! You're far too busy eating
ice cream all year round!

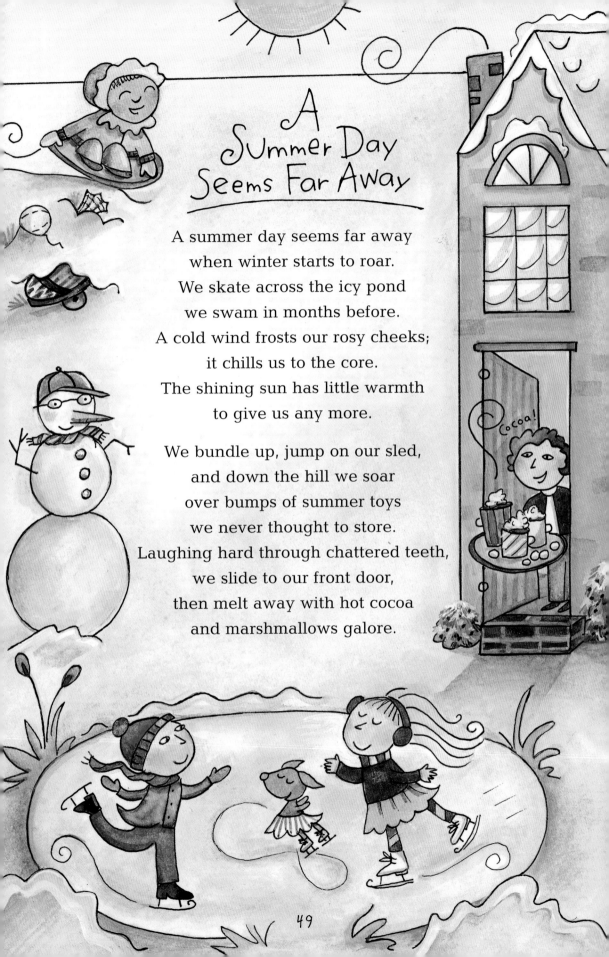

A Summer Day Seems Far Away

A summer day seems far away
when winter starts to roar.
We skate across the icy pond
we swam in months before.
A cold wind frosts our rosy cheeks;
it chills us to the core.
The shining sun has little warmth
to give us any more.

We bundle up, jump on our sled,
and down the hill we soar
over bumps of summer toys
we never thought to store.
Laughing hard through chattered teeth,
we slide to our front door,
then melt away with hot cocoa
and marshmallows galore.

Faith Prayer Alms-giving Fasting Pilgrimage

5 Pillars of Islam

Ninth Month of the Muslim Calendar

Ramadan Has Begun

Ramadan has begun,
    So don't wake the sun
        Until after our suhur is served.
Not a sip nor a bite
    Till the day turns to night
        And the prayers of our faith are observed.
Ramadan will end soon
    With the new crescent moon,
        So we give to the ones who have least.
Happy neighbors prepare
    Meats and sweets they will share
        At the fast-breaking festival feast!

suhur

Alms for Poor

Holy Koran

It's Hanukkah!

In December, we remember Maccabees, so brave and bold.

By our lighting this menorah

Oil for one day,

In December,

we remember

lasting eight—

and by the latkes on our plate.

For eight days we open presents, spinning dreidels, winning gold!

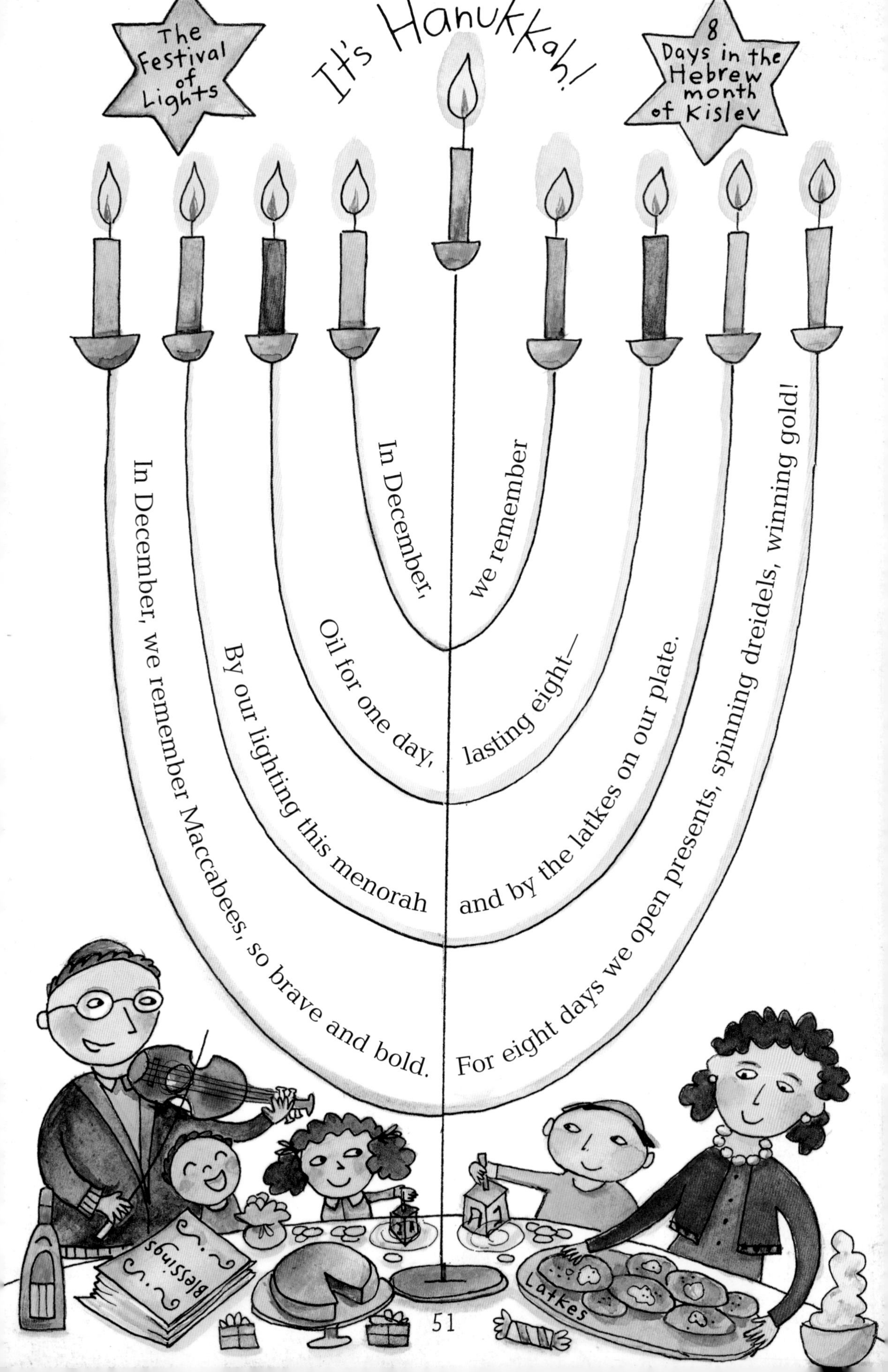

Blessings

Latkes

51

The Nativity "Seen"

If I were alive when Jesus was born,
would I be a shepherd or king?
As a king, I could ride on a camel, up high,
with gifts of fine treasures to bring.
As a shepherd, I would be the poorest of poor,
but, imagine, I'd hear angels sing!

A shepherd or king? Both one and the same
to the baby asleep on the hay,
For all in the stable (the animals, too!)
were blessed that Nativity day.

Our Family Treasure Chest

Around the world, how can it be
That every single Christmas tree
Is decorated differently?

Up the attic stairs we creep,
Down go boxes where we keep
Our ornaments all tucked asleep.

As tissue crinkles, tales unfold
About the treasures that we hold—
The handmade new, the hand-down old.

And though we've heard these tales before,
We keep unwrapping to hear more . . .
We keep unwrapping to hear more.

Department Store

Share

For the Poor

Apply Here

Hospital

Entrance

Me? shhh — I'm a secret Santa!

Santas, Santas Everywhere

Santas, Santas everywhere,
but how can that be so?
They stand on every corner
from Vermont to Idaho.
Could Santa have a dozen cousins
with the last name Claus?
Do tall elves work a second shift
to help a worthy cause?

He must be pretty picky picking
out his substitutes.
They all look nice and jolly
in their big red Santa suits.
Well, maybe it's okay to see
these Santas everywhere.
They all must have some Santa Claus
inside of them to share.

Santa's Helper Application
To apply for this very important position,
please check where appropriate:

— Eyes that sparkle
— Will say "ho ho ho" not "ho hee" or "ha"
— Kind smile
— Will not wear Santa suit in the summer
— White beard
— Can spell hard words, like Tyrannosaurus rex
— Good listener
— Has two short friends willing to hand out candy canes (and wear green tights)

SANTA Letters

Dear Santa,
If you'll re-read my letter,
I never mentioned "sweater."

This new coat may be warmer,
but it's no "Bug Transformer."

A scarf with Christmas trees
won't need new batteries.

I'm thinking toys are best.
Aunt Ruth will bring the rest.

Thank you for the thought, though.
Sincerely, Bob Legotto

Dear Santa,
When you come to my house,
could you give me a lift?
I need to deliver
my best friend a gift.
I figure you're probably
heading that way
and might like some company
up in the sleigh.
Love, Bailey

Santa,
My candy cane has disappeared!
Remember when I tugged your beard?
If you find it, send it quick!
I think it may have one more lick!
Your friend, Chelsea

Dear Santa, dear Santa,
It's Billy from Maine.
I'm writing this letter
so I can explain:
I didn't know noodles
could stick to long hair
or grapes could escape—
I just wasn't aware.

I'm still on your good list—
you understand, right?
A boy has to learn
not to start a food fight.
I'll try to be good, Santa,
starting today.
I think there is time—
it's the fifteenth of May.
From Billy

Dear Santa,
If you're free after Christmas
(and I'm thinking you are),
while the reindeer are resting,
can you borrow a car?
Drive south to my school
for Career Day in May—
you sure have the job
that I want someday!
From Chris

SOUTH

55

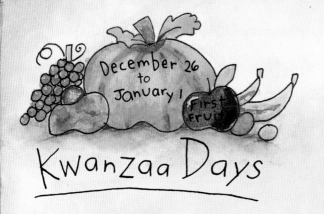

December 26
to
January 1
First Fruit

Kwanzaa Days

In the seven mornings,
  Greet me with *Habari gani?*
And I will try to answer
  Umoja or *Imani.*

During the seven days,
  Lay out the *mkeka* and cup.
And I will count the *muhindi*
  And gifts that you wrap up.

In the seven evenings,
  Light the candles: red, black, green.
And I will grow up knowing
  What my African roots mean.

Seven Principles
(in Swahili)
1) Umoja (Unity)
2) Kujichagulia
(self-determination)
3) Ujima
  (working together)
4) Ujamaa
(cooperative economics)
5) Nia (purpose)
6) Kuumba
  (creativity)
7) Imani (faith)

Jambo!
(hello)

Habari gani?
(what's new?)

Imani!

Unity Cup

Kinara
(candle holder)

muhindi
(corn)

mkeka
(straw mat)

On New Year's Eve

What happens at midnight
On New Year's Eve?
We kids will never know.

Each year it's the same—
We fall asleep
With minutes left to go.

We can only imagine
What we must miss
That makes the grown-ups cheer.

Shooting stars?
Colored snow?
Magical elves?
Wake us! Oh, wake us next year!

The Weather Report
(On Groundhog Day)

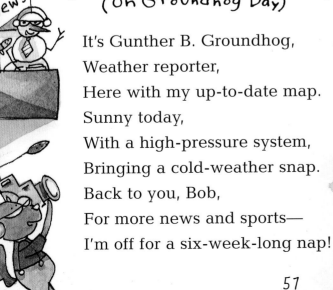

It's Gunther B. Groundhog,
Weather reporter,
Here with my up-to-date map.
Sunny today,
With a high-pressure system,
Bringing a cold-weather snap.
Back to you, Bob,
For more news and sports—
I'm off for a six-week-long nap!

Celebrating Chinese New Year

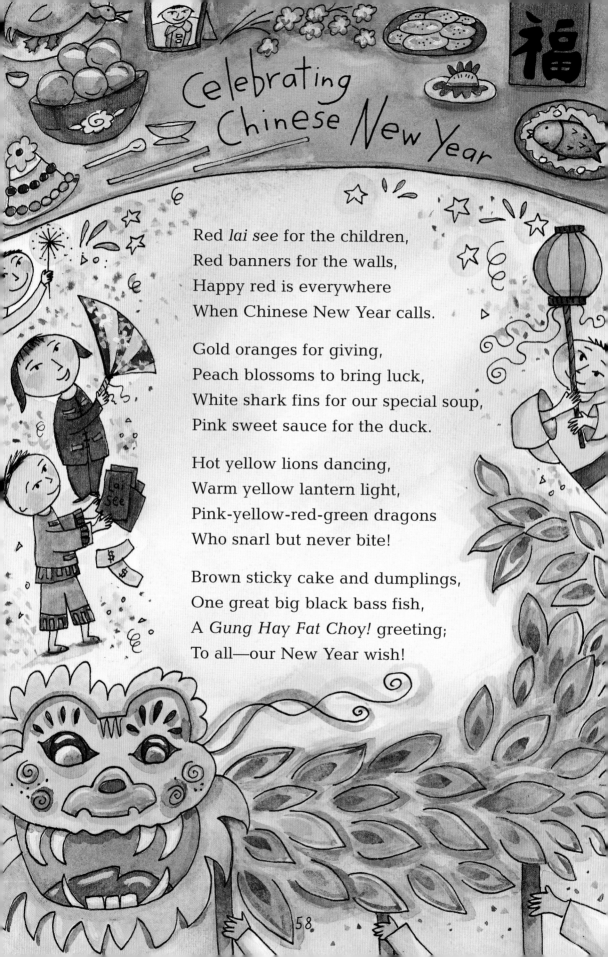

Red *lai see* for the children,
Red banners for the walls,
Happy red is everywhere
When Chinese New Year calls.

Gold oranges for giving,
Peach blossoms to bring luck,
White shark fins for our special soup,
Pink sweet sauce for the duck.

Hot yellow lions dancing,
Warm yellow lantern light,
Pink-yellow-red-green dragons
Who snarl but never bite!

Brown sticky cake and dumplings,
One great big black bass fish,
A *Gung Hay Fat Choy!* greeting;
To all—our New Year wish!

In Honor of Dr. Martin Luther King

Who said "NO MORE!" to prejudice
And laws that were unfair?
Who said "NO MORE!" without a fight
In peaceful words and prayer?
Who said "NO MORE!" and showed the world
What love, not hate, could bring?
The one the world will not forget—
Martin Luther King.

3rd Monday in January

A dream's just a dream
If it stays in your head.
Shout it and share it
And live it instead!

I have a DREAM

On Presidents' Day

On behalf of the presidents honored today,

We turn to our nation's next leaders and say,

Children, work hard in whatever you do,

Then you can grow up to be president, also!

3rd Monday in Feb.

No, no, Abe—president, TOO!

Oh, Abe, we've been working on this for years!

WOW

59

How to Make a Valentine
by Bobby

Cut one red heart,
Sprinkle sprinkles,
Smoosh out all the
Glue-bump wrinkles.
Stick some stickers,
Scribble,
Swirl swirl.
Give to Grandma,
Not a GIRL girl.
(No way!)

I grew up a shoe box
With only one job—
To carry your new pair of shoes.
But look at me now—
A fancy red box
Covered in glitter and glue.

It's Valentine's Day—
I'm going to school!
I sit on your lap on the bus.
Soon I'm a mailbox
With a new job—
Hold valentines given to us.

And on the way home
You read every note,
Returning your favorites to me.
Then back in the closet
I start the best job—
Preserving this memory.

Match the ♥ with the animal!

ANIMAL CANDY HEARTS

$2.00

Perfect for:

Cats
Squirrels
Skunks
Fish
Bees
Porcupines
Frogs
Lightning bugs
Spiders
Bears

I'm nutty about you!

How well you smell!

You put the zing in my sting!

You put the OWWW in my growl.

Meet me at Lover's Leap.

You're a dish of a fish!

You light my fire!

You give me the creeps. Wow!

I'm smitten, kitten.

You put the fine in my pine!

Follow your instincts and buy this box!

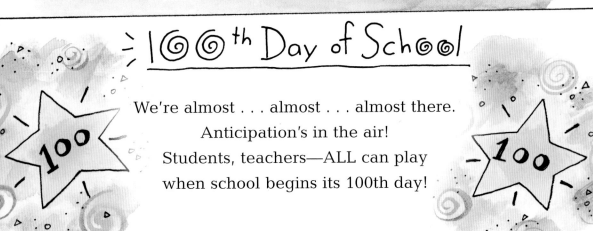

100th Day of School

We're almost . . . almost . . . almost there.
Anticipation's in the air!
Students, teachers—ALL can play
when school begins its 100th day!

100

100

My Birthday Wish List
(very affordable!)

1. One homemade sign taped to my chair.
2. Two streamers twisting in the air.
3. Three chocolate pancakes in a stack.
4. Four hugs (and I'll give four hugs back).
5. Five cards that I find all day long.
6. Six friends singing the birthday song.
7. Seven cake-smearing belly laughs.
8. Eight face-frosting photographs.
9. Nine striped birthday horns that whine.
10. Ten gifts, of course, would be just fine.

(But don't forget my one through nine!)

Happy Birthday

Growing Pains!

If a birthday pinch
Makes you grow an inch,
How did I get so tall?
One inch a year's
Not much, I fear.
I should be one foot small!

A Season for Birthdays

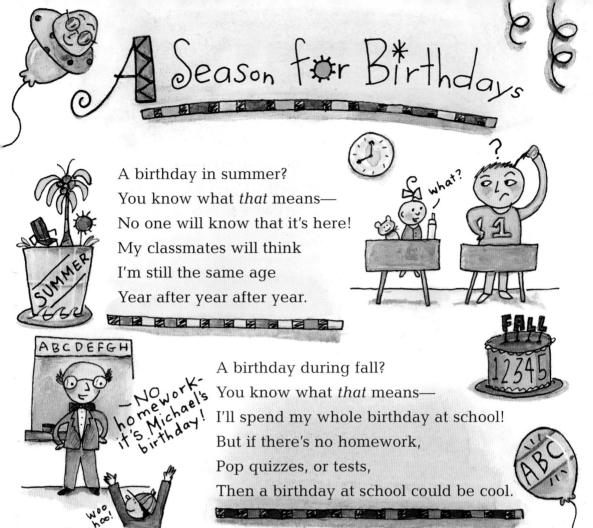

A birthday in summer?
You know what *that* means—
No one will know that it's here!
My classmates will think
I'm still the same age
Year after year after year.

A birthday during fall?
You know what *that* means—
I'll spend my whole birthday at school!
But if there's no homework,
Pop quizzes, or tests,
Then a birthday at school could be cool.

A birthday in winter?
You know what *that* means—
No gifts for the rest of the year!
ChristmasKwanzaaBirthday
BUMP!
Too fast! Too close! Too near!

A birthday during spring?
You know what that means—
I may have to share my big day
With leprechauns, presidents,
Bunnies, my mom—
Hmm . . . I guess that'd be okay.

End-of-Year Party!

As host of our end-of-year party, I say,
"We did it again! Great job, all! Hooray!
No need for name tags—we've been friends for years.
Relax and eat hearty, my dear volunteers.
It's so great to see you, but now I must run . . .
You know that a tooth fairy's job's never done!"

64